WHEN THE Dragons CAME

To our fabulous husbands, Mike and Simon,
for all their support and encouragement,
and to Archie, Charlie, Joe and Will, our wonderful boys,
whose passion for dragons sparked this story – **NK/LM**

For Mum and Dad – **BD**

SIMON & SCHUSTER
First published in Great Britain in 2010
This special edition published in 2021 by Simon & Schuster UK Ltd
1st Floor, 222 Gray's Inn Road, London WC1X 8HB

Text copyright © 2010 Naomi Kefford and Lynne Moore
Illustrations copyright © 2010 Benji Davies

The right of Naomi Kefford, Lynne Moore and Benji Davies to be identified as
the authors and illustrator of this work has been asserted by them in accordance
with the Copyright, Designs and Patents Act, 1988

ISBN: 978-1-4711-4427-1
Printed in China
1 3 5 7 9 10 8 6 4 2

WHEN THE Dragons CAME

Naomi Kefford and Lynne Moore
Illustrated by Benji Davies

SIMON & SCHUSTER
London   New York   Sydney   Toronto   New Delhi

Poppledown Town was the loveliest town.

The neat rows of houses had charming front gardens,
With hedges and lawns that were trimmed every day.
The High Street provided whatever was needed,
The riverbank was perfect for picnics in May.

Oh yes,
Poppledown Town was the LOVELIEST town.
And everyone that lived there agreed.

Amelia Topping loved shopping.

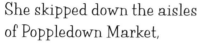

She skipped down the aisles
of Poppledown Market,

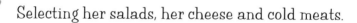

Selecting her salads, her cheese and cold meats.

She paused at the freezers and chose all her favourites,
Then filled up her trolley with doughnuts and treats.

Oh yes,
Amelia Topping LOVED shopping...

...until the **dragons** came!

SPECIAL OFFER

Fredrick Fielding loved reading.

He hurried each morning to Poppledown Library,
Treasuring the hush as he browsed along rows.

He liked choosing stories and reading them quietly,
And the click of the stamp on each book that he chose.

Oh yes,
Fredrick Fielding LOVED reading . . .

...until the dragons came!

Olivia Turning loved learning.

She sat on the carpet at
Poppledown Playgroup,

Eager for stories and songs with Miss Twee.

She carefully moulded her plasticine biscuits,
Ready to use in her Teddy Bears' Tea.

Oh yes,
Olivia Turning LOVED learning . . .

...until the dragons came!

So Olivia Turning HATED learning,
Fredrick Fielding AVOIDED reading,
And Amelia Topping STOPPED shopping,

For Poppledown Town just wasn't the same,
since the dragons came.

But . . .

Jeremy Stamping LOVED camping.

He set up his tent on Poppledown Common,
A holiday village of orange and red.

He checked all the guy ropes, the pegs and the zippers,
Then sizzled his sausages and pumped up his bed.

Oh yes,
Jeremy Stamping LOVED camping . . .

...until the **rain** came!

It drummed on the canvas like zebras tap-dancing,
It hammered the flysheet and trickled down poles.

It seeped into sleeping bags, gathered in puddles.
The campers were soggy and hungry and cold . . .

. . . until the

dragons came!

They spread out their wings and provided a shelter,
They dried up the puddles, cooked sausages to share.
The campers saw kindness and talked with the dragons,
They realised quite quickly they HAD NOT BEEN FAIR!

They explained to the dragons just how they'd annoyed them,
With clumsy behaviour and the mess that they'd made.
The dragons said sorry, they'd meant to be friendly.
They'd try to be careful and calm if they stayed . . .

So Olivia Turning went BACK to her learning,

Fredrick Fielding CONTINUED reading,

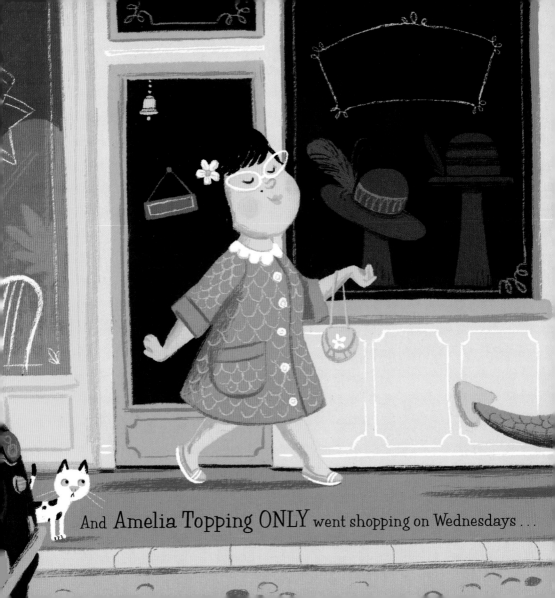

And Amelia Topping ONLY went shopping on Wednesdays...

. . . when the **dragons** came!